HAVE A *SAFE* HOLIDAY

Sheriff

CELEBRATE RESPONSIBLY

WISHING YOU A FABULOUS HOLIDAY!

TWIN H-POWER

Doc

Have a *Stylin'* holiday!

Flo & Ramone

ATTEN-HUT!

HAVE A MERRY CHRISTMAS!

SARGE

AND THAT'S AN ORDER, SOLDIER!

To Joe Ranft, for the inspiration
and for Eden, Bosco, and Beach

Printed in the United States of America

First Edition

3 5 7 9 10 8 6 4

Library of Congress Cataloging-in-Publication Data on file.

ISBN 973-1-4231-1695-0

Visit www.disneybooks.com

G942-9090-6 10166

SUSTAINABLE FORESTRY INITIATIVE

Certified Chain of Custody
40% Certified Forests,
60% Certified Fiber Sourcing

www.sfiprogram.org

PWC-SFICOC-260

This Label Applies To Text Pages Only

Disney · PIXAR

MATER SAVES CHRISTMAS

Written by Kiel Murray

Based on a story by John Lasseter

Illustrations by The Disney Storybook Artists

Disney PRESS
New York

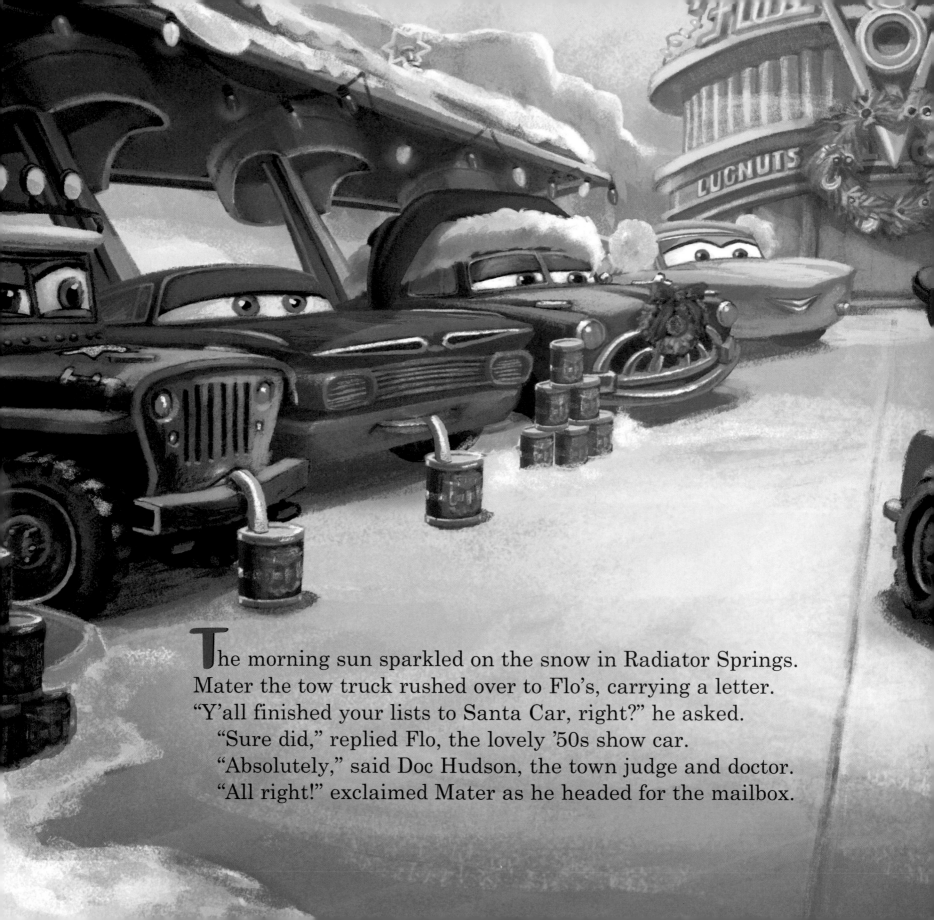

The morning sun sparkled on the snow in Radiator Springs. Mater the tow truck rushed over to Flo's, carrying a letter. "Y'all finished your lists to Santa Car, right?" he asked.

"Sure did," replied Flo, the lovely '50s show car.

"Absolutely," said Doc Hudson, the town judge and doctor.

"All right!" exclaimed Mater as he headed for the mailbox.

Mater was just about to mail his letter when he heard a familiar voice.

"Come on, Mater, surely even you know that Santa Car isn't real," said Chick Hicks.

"Next you're gonna tell me that the Easter Buggy don't exist neither," Mater said. Then he dropped his letter into the mailbox.

"What are you doing here, Chick?"
asked Lightning McQueen suspiciously.
"Oh, hey, Lightning, didn't see ya there.
I just came by to donate to Red's Toy
Drive," replied Chick.

Lightning frowned. He was sure that
Chick was up to no good.

Just then, Sheriff arrived. "I'm afraid I have some bad news, folks. Fill-up stations up and down the route have been robbed. All the gas has been stolen!"

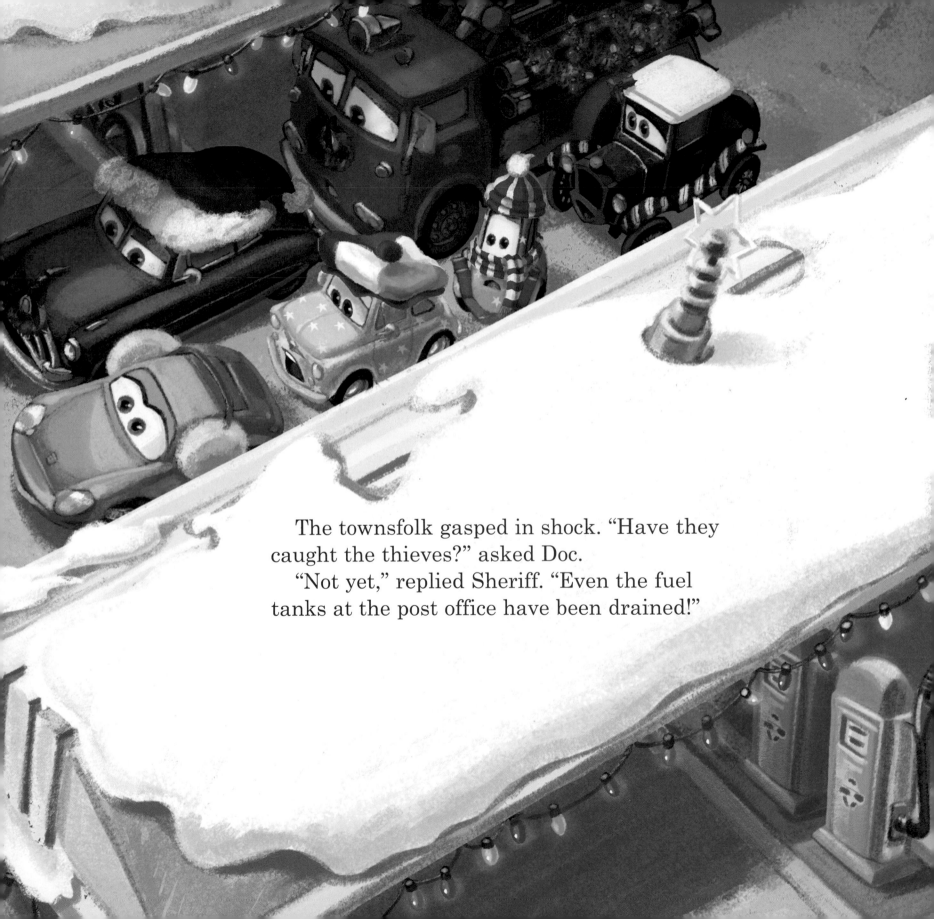

The townsfolk gasped in shock. "Have they caught the thieves?" asked Doc.

"Not yet," replied Sheriff. "Even the fuel tanks at the post office have been drained!"

"Without gas, the mail trucks can't get through! That means the letters won't get to Santa Car! That means no Christmas!" Mater cried.

Mater immediately drove over to the gas pump.
"Fill 'er up, Flo. I'll go to the North Pole and take
the letters to Santa Car myself!" he declared.
"I'm tryin'," said Flo, "but there's no gas!"

Sure enough, Flo's place had been robbed, too!
Mater narrowed his eyes at Chick, who was
chuckling with his friends.

Fillmore, the hippie van, whispered to Mater,
"Meet me at the dome in five."

When Mater got to the dome,
Fillmore filled the tow truck's tank
with the last of his Christmas brew.
Mater was thrilled.

Fillmore made Mater promise to put his letter
on the top of the pile for Santa Car. "Never stop
believin', man!" he said.

Back at Flo's, Mater got ready to head out with
the letters, but the townsfolk were worried, especially
Lightning. He couldn't let Mater go alone. He knew
what he had to do.

"Mater, I'm going with you," Lightning said.

"But you can't!" exclaimed Mater. "You don't even have snow tires!"

"Did somebody say tires?" said Luigi, the yellow Fiat.

Just as if Lightning were in a race, Guido, the Italian forklift, gave him a quick pit stop.

Then Sarge, the army jeep, added some snow
gear of his own. . . .

BIG LIGHTS!

SNOWPLOW!

FOG LAMPS!

"Now that's what I call good lookin'! North Pole,
here we come!" Mater exclaimed.

"*Oh, timing belt, oh, timing belt, how lovely is yer rubber. . . .*" Mater sang as he and Lightning started their long journey to the North Pole.

NORTH POLE

The two friends made their way through deep snow and tough terrain. Lightning was tired, but Mater's spirits remained high. *"Frosty the snow plow..."* he sang. "Come on, buddy, sing it with me!"

Back in town, Sheriff came up with a plan to find the fuel thieves. Luigi and Guido would be scouts. Sally was in charge of maps, and Fillmore would make fuel to keep the search party going.

Moments later, Fillmore discovered that his fuel-making supplies had been stolen! Now he wouldn't be able to fuel the townsfolk for the hunt.

Luckily, Sarge had a plan. "Buck up, soldiers, we'll pool our remaining fuel for Luigi and Guido, and they'll track the thieves," he said.

Way up north, Mater and Lightning were exhausted. They both sang carols to keep themselves awake. *"All I want for Christmas is my two front tires. My two front—"*

BONK!

All of a sudden, Mater hit a candy-striped pole. "The North Pole! We found it, buddy!" shouted Mater.

It was the North Pole all right, and it was beautiful!
Snow-covered garages lined the paths, tiny elf cars bustled
about, and in the center of it all was Santa Car himself.

Mater was overjoyed. Lightning stared in amazement.
"Santa Car *is* real!" the race car said.

"Welcome to the North Pole, gentlemen," said Santa Car.

Santa Car was glad that his new friends had brought their letters all this way, but he had some bad news. "Christmas may be cancelled this year," he said.

"No Christmas?!" cried Mater.

"The reindeer snowmobiles that fly me around the world have been stolen," said Santa Car.

Just then, Mater remembered Chick and his friends acting suspiciously at Flo's. "Chick Hicks took your reindeer!" he cried.

"The reindeer are fed top secret fuel that helps them fly," said Santa Car.

"The fuel! That's why he took them!" exclaimed Lightning. "Chick will do anything to win a race."

"I'd tow you down to Radiator Springs to find yer reindeer, Mr. Santa Car, but we'd never make it in time to save Christmas," offered Mater.

But Santa Car had a better idea. He filled Mater's tank with the special flying fuel!

As Mater prepared to tow Santa Car to Radiator Springs, he proudly showed off the antler hat that Mrs. Santa Car had knit him for the journey.

Back in Ornament Valley, Luigi and Guido scouted the canyons for the fuel thieves. From a cliff, they spotted Chick and his posse making fuel with Fillmore's supplies! Santa Car's reindeer snowmobiles were there, too!

All of a sudden, two of Chick's pals cornered Guido and Luigi.

"Ha! You're too late, boys!" Chick shouted at Guido and Luigi. "We already reverse-engineered the flying fuel. I'll fly around the track and never lose to Lightning McQueen again! And you know the best part? No more Christmas! No more dirty oil filters in my stocking! If I can't have presents, no one can!"

Suddenly, the air was filled with the sound of jingling bells. Then, Mater soared over the hill, towing Lightning and Santa Car.

Chick raced away, flying just above the ground. Lightning flew after him. Santa Car had filled his tank with the magic fuel back at the North Pole!

Meanwhile, Sheriff and the townsfolk followed Guido's and Luigi's tracks right to Chick's posse. They set Guido, Luigi, and the reindeer free!

Chick was flying fast, but he was no match for Lightning, who knew each turn by heart. As Chick came to a sharp curve, he turned too late, smacked into a giant cactus, and spun out of control.

Doc and Mater joined Lightning on the cliff to take a look at the wreckage.

"Have fun fishin', Mater," said Doc. "Tow him straight to jail."

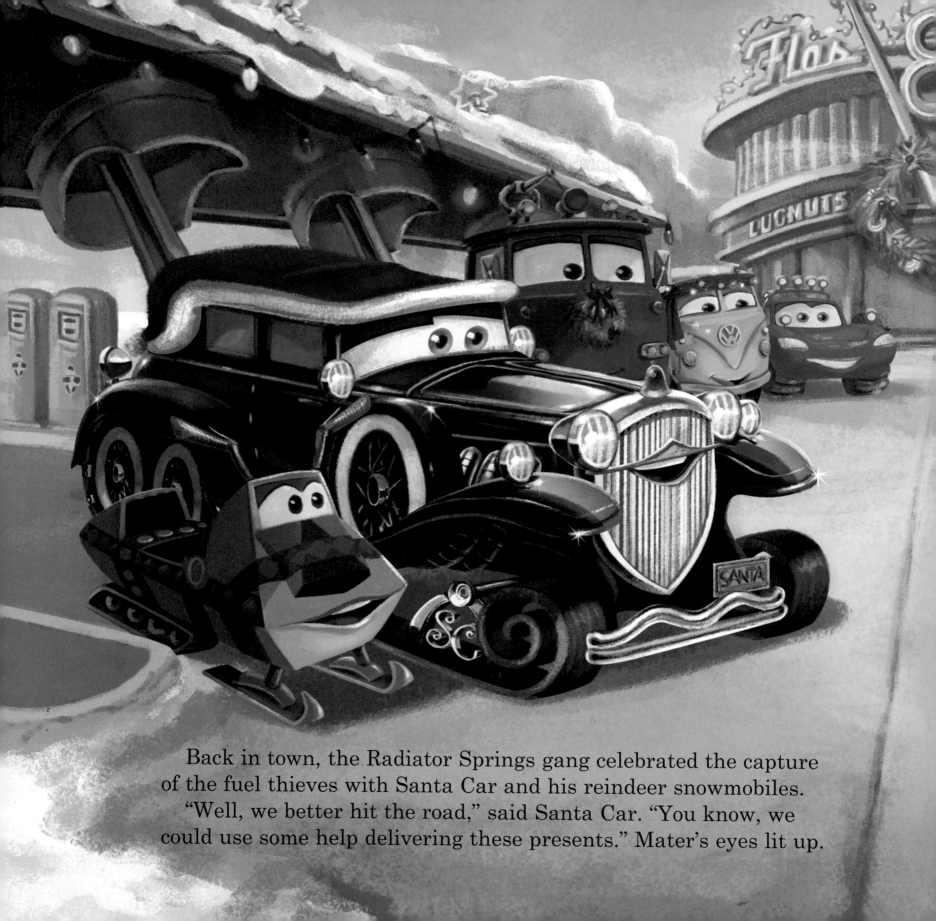

Back in town, the Radiator Springs gang celebrated the capture of the fuel thieves with Santa Car and his reindeer snowmobiles. "Well, we better hit the road," said Santa Car. "You know, we could use some help delivering these presents." Mater's eyes lit up.

"What do you say, Mater? Will you help me bring
Christmas?" asked Santa Car.
"Sure thing!" yelled Mater. "Let's get 'er done!"
The townsfolk all cheered. Mater had saved Christmas!

Merry Christmas tow all, and tow all a good night!